This
PJ BOOK
belongs to

PJLibrary®

JEWISH BEDTIME STORIES and SONGS

On Sunday, "La-lee-la-lo-lair,"
The Cricket chirped in the town square.

On Monday, *"Chit-chat-chit-chat-chark,"*
The Cricket warbled in the park.

On Tuesday, oh! How very sweet,
"Tra-la, tra-la," trilled in the street.

On Wednesday, *"Diddle-dum, dum-dee,"*
He leaped and danced along the sea.

On Thursday, *"Yoppity-yippety-yop,"*
He sang and played at a nearby shop.

The week had been busy with singing and fun
And Cricket was tired from all he had done.

So on Friday morning, he opened one eye—
"Oh, it's too early," he said with a sigh.
"I'll sleep a bit longer and then when I wake
I'll bake for Shabbat a yum-yummy cake."

He woke a bit later… "Just one hour more,"
He said in a voice that turned into a snore.

Then he woke with a start and sprang from his bed!
He stared at the clock. "Oh, where was my head?
It's late afternoon. I've no time to waste.
Shabbat's coming soon. I must bake with haste!"

He rushed to the pantry, then gasped, "Oh, dear me!"
There was nothing—no crumb! No food he could see.

He dashed to the fridge and peeked in—but once more
There was nothing inside when he opened the door.
He searched all the cupboards to hunt and to check
But his whole house was bare—not one nibble or speck.

The Cricket was stumped. "Now what can I do?
There's no time to shop for more groceries, it's true.
So how will I make my grand Shabbat cake?
Could I use some fine sand, plus some drops from the lake?"

Then he sniffed at the air. "Hang on—what's that smell?
Something yummy is baking nearby, I can tell.
Someone is making a cake while I can't.
It must be that hardworking insect, the Ant."

So the Cricket went knocking upon the Ant's door.
"Excuse me, but could I just trouble you for...
One small spoon of sugar? I'm baking, you see—
At least I *will* bake, if there's sugar for me."

"Thank you so kindly," he said, and rushed back.
But then in his kitchen, "Oh no! Now I lack..."

knock-knock-knock

"Hello again, Ant. I'm back. If I may—
Can you spare me a droplet of oil today?"
He bowed to the ant, then he hopped, and rushed back,
He entered his kitchen, "Oh no! Now I lack . . ."

knock-knock-knock

"Madam Ant, just once more I must beg.
Could you spare for a cricket just half of an egg?
Thank you, dear Ant, you're a fine friend indeed."
He rushed to his kitchen, "Do I have all I need?"

knock-knock-knock

"Sorry, I just need some flour, a bit,
A handful, a pinch—yes, thank you, that's it."

The Ant heaved a sigh but then said, "Indeed,
It's pleasant to help out a friend who's in need."

Then the Ant, in her chair, lay back, closed her eyes,
Just as the moon was beginning to rise.
But what, you may ask, of her wonderful cake?
Did she turn off her oven? No?? *What* a mistake!

All of a sudden she gasped and awoke.
The kitchen was filled with a grey cloud of smoke!
She glanced at the oven. Her stomach had turned.
Oh no! Her Shabbat cake was totally burned!

Her table was set with wine red and sweet,
The candles, the challah —but no cake to eat.
Ant sighed and she felt that her heart just might break,
For how could she welcome Shabbat without cake?

She tasted some soup, took a sip, took a bite.
She chewed and she swallowed with no appetite.
When all of a sudden . . . *KNOCK-KNOCK* at the door.
"Who could it be?" she thought, crossing the floor.

It's the Cricket, all smiles! And what's on his tray?
A cake for Shabbat, for this most special day!
"My dear friend," said Cricket, as he pulled out a chair.
"I've baked us this cake that I hope you will share."

Side by side at the table, the Cricket and Ant
Clink their glasses together. "L'chaim!" they chant.
They sing and they dance, and their joy has no end.
Let's welcome Shabbat with the Ant and her friend!

Naomi Ben-Gur is a writer, translator, editor and a professor of children's literature. Born in Tel Aviv, Israel, she served as a military correspondent in the IDF. At the age of 19, while serving in the Israeli army, she published her first book of poems. Naomi earned a B.A. in Literature from Tel Aviv University, a Master's degree in Cinema Studies from New York University and a Ph.D in Comparative Literature from the Hebrew University of Jerusalem. She has written over 40 children's books and is also a children's book editor for Hakibbutz Hameuchad-Sifriat Poalim Publishing Group. She lives in Tel Aviv.

Shahar Kober is a graduate of Shenkar College of Design in Israel. He has illustrated over 30 children's books including Kar-Ben's popular "Engineer Ari" series. His work has been published in the United States, Israel, France, the United Kingdom and other countries. Shahar lives with his wife, two sons, dog and cat in Kiryat Tivon, Israel.